Public SPEECH MARKS

Dear Reader

Have you had to give a speech to your class or your school? It is an honour to be asked to give a speech.

When I was at school, I felt a bit nervous when I was first asked to make a speech. But after I learnt how to plan and present a speech, I really enjoyed doing it.

ENJOY MAKING A SPEECH BY PLANNING AND PRACTISING IT FIRST.

In this book, I created two dalmatian characters – KIng and Queen Dalmatian – to help you learn more about making speeches. The characters have a lot of fun "telling" you what to do, and I hope you have fun, too!

I hope you enjoy reading about making and writing speeches as much as I enjoyed researching this topic!

Sharon Parsons

Contents

PUBLIC Speech Marks

1 Superheroes' Welcome Speech

Imagine the Speech First

The Task

Imagine you and your friend are the main characters in an end-of-year school play. You have been asked to make a speech to welcome parents, families and friends to the play.

The Play

The play is called, *109 Superhero Dalmatians*. It will be based on the popular story of *101 Dalmatians*.

Main Characters

You and your friend are "**King Dalmatian**" and "**Queen Dalmatian**". You are supreme superheroes.

Humour

Think about what kind of fun and humour you could include in the speech.

Character Voice

Think about the kind of voice you would use.

Other Characters

The other 107 dalmatians are only superheroes.

Character Make-up

Imagine what make-up you would wear.

Character Costume

Imagine what your character would wear.

Act in Character

Write your speech in the character of the king and the queen.

Character Movement

Think about how a dalmatian character would move.

2 Stuck on a Speech?

Think **Before** You Read

Think about each question before you read the answers. Question 5 will help you understand the welcome speech on pages 8 to 10.

Q1

Why should there be a welcome speech before a school play?

A1

Speeches can:

- welcome parents, families, friends and teachers
- thank people who helped with the play
- tell everyone about the play
- wish everyone a great night.

Q2

How long should a welcome speech be?

A2

About two minutes long.

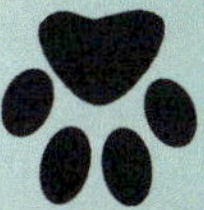

Q3

Where should you stand for your welcome speech?

A3

King Dalmatian sits beside his throne and Queen Dalmatian sits on her throne.

Q4

How should your superhero characters speak?

A4

Practise how you think your character would speak. You might use a deep, scary voice or a high, happy voice.

Q5

What should you say in a welcome speech?

A5

Most speeches are like stories. They have:

- a beginning
- a middle
- an ending.

Read **Before** You Write

First, read this idea for a welcome speech for the play *109 Superhero Dalmatians*. As you read it, think about what you could write for your welcome speech.

The Beginning of the Speech

Queen Dalmatian:
Good evening everyone! Thank you for coming tonight. Meet the Spotty Kingster.

King Dalmatian:
The Spotty Kingster? I told you not to call me that!

Queen Dalmatian:
As I was saying, we want to welcome you to our school play, *109 Superhero Dalmatians*.

King Dalmatian:
Grrr, yes, we welcome you. And, grrr, we want to thank our teachers and parents for helping us with our play.

The Middle of the Speech

Queen Dalmatian:
The play is our adaptation of the story, *101 Dalmatians*. We have some extra kids from Year 4, so that's why we have 109 dalmatians!

King Dalmatian:
Grrr, but let me tell you, the other 107 dalmatians are just superheroes. The Meany Queeny and I are thc supreme superhero dalmatians with our superhero spots.

Lights shine on all the other dalmatian characters who laugh behind the King and the Queen.

Queen Dalmatian:
Meany Queeny? I told you not to call me that! Anyway, in the story, evil Rotter Rottweiler steals our superhero spots. The spots hold our superhero powers and so he becomes more powerful than us. Grrr! The play gets exciting when we find more superhero spots to overpower the Rotter Rottweiler in our queendom.

The End of the Speech

King Dalmatian:
Surely you mean kingdom, dear? Anyway, we hope you enjoy our play. Grrr … where are my doggie treats, Queenie?

Queen Dalmatian looks guilty and glances at the audience.

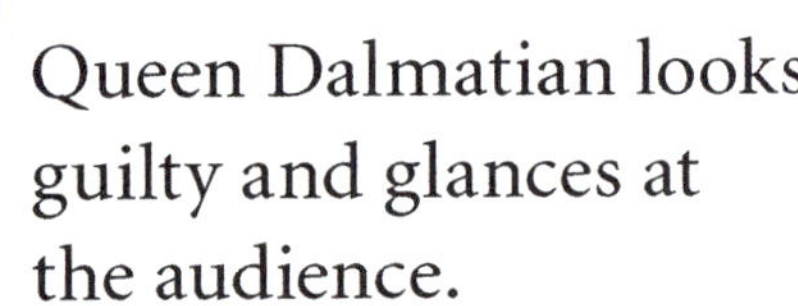

King Dalmatian:
What? Are MY treats under everyone's seats?

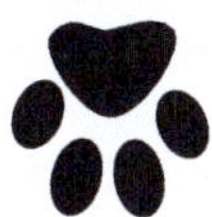

Some wrapped-up biscuits have been put under the chairs of the audience. It's their treat!

Arts and History

101 Dalmatians' History

The book The Hundred and One Dalmatians was written by Dodie Smith in 1956. Five years later, Walt Disney made an animated film about it called One Hundred and One Dalmatians.

In 1996, a live-action movie called 101 Dalmatians was released. For that movie, over 200 dalmatian puppies were trained for the many scenes!

Dodie Smith, author of The Hundred and One Dalmatians *at home with a dalmatian.*

Review: *109 Superhero Dalmatians* Welcome Speech

You've Got **Mail!**

Imagine that the school play – *109 Superhero Dalmatians* – is over. A letter arrives from the President of the Parents' Association. It is addressed to the King and Queen Superhero Dalmatians. This letter is a polite way of saying thank you for the play. In the letter, the writer includes a review. It tells the reader what they thought of the welcome speech.

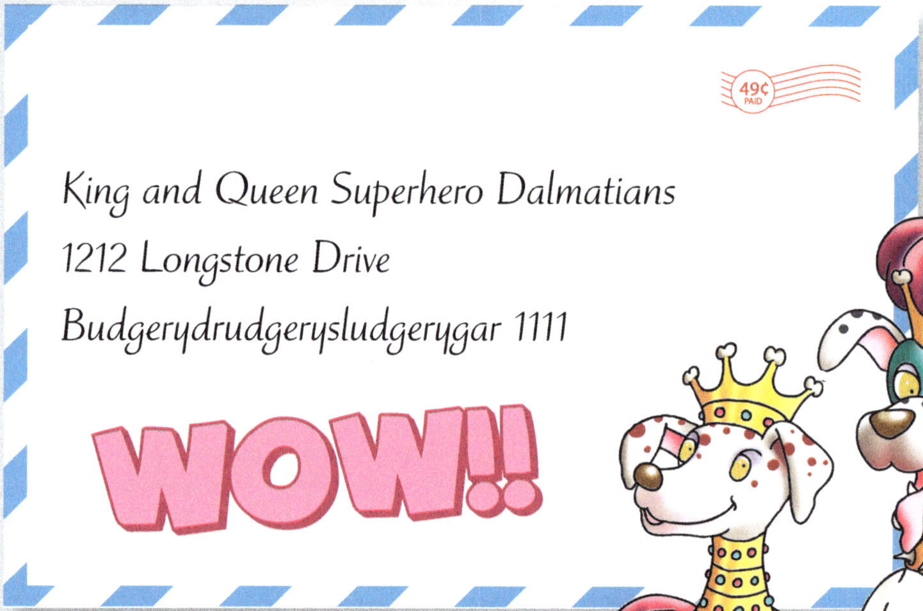

49¢ PAID

King and Queen Superhero Dalmatians
1212 Longstone Drive
Budgerydrudgerysludgerygar 1111

WOW!!

TEXT TYPE
Response

Tuesday 1 December 2010

King and Queen Superhero Dalmatians

1212 Longstone Drive

Budgerydrudgerysludgerygar 1111

Dear King and Queen Superhero Dalmatians,

On behalf of the Parents' Association, I want to thank you both for a great speech at the start of your play, 109 Superhero Dalmatians. Here are some of the reasons why we thought it was an excellent speech:

- First, the speech was very well written. Also, it wasn't too long.
- You had practised your speech. You did not need to look down at your notes very much.
- Your speech was entertaining to watch.
- You dressed up as dalmatian characters and you looked like you were having fun.
- We heard every word you said because you spoke very clearly.
- Finally, your speech got us very excited about the play. It was one of the best school plays we have ever seen!

Our thanks to you and the other 107 dalmatian characters. All the parents and friends enjoyed the play. We look forward to your next speech.

Regards,
Jennifer Smithson
President of the Parents' Association

PS Thanks for the biscuits!

4 Top Three Speech Ideas

Words + Voice + Body Language = **a Speech**

First Idea for a Speech:

Your Words

Your words – what you want to say in your speech – are the first things to think about.

Key Things to Do

Research: Find out who your audience is and what they need to hear in your speech.

Be concise: Write your speech with as few words as you can.

Entertain: Think of one or two ways to add humour or interest to your speech for your audience.

Write your speech like a story, with a beginning, a middle and an ending.

Beginning: The beginning is also called the speech's "introduction". It is where you introduce yourself and your topic to your audience.

Middle: The middle is also called the speech's "body". It is where you describe your main points.

Ending: The ending is also called the speech's "conclusion". It is where you summarise what you have said. You should also thank your audience for their attention.

CLEAR VOICE

2

Second Idea for a Speech:

Your Voice

Your voice is the second most important thing to think about. These points will help you.

A clear speaking voice: pronounce or say your words clearly.

A voice that can be heard: make your voice louder if you're in a large room or outside.

A voice that doesn't rush: think about when to slow down your speech so the audience has time to understand your message.

A voice that uses the right tone: change the tone of your voice when you make important points.

Quotation Marks

"Quotation marks" are the punctuation marks that show the beginning and the end of speech. Sometimes they are also called speech marks.

“ ”

A voice that sounds confident: your speech will sound more interesting if you practise speaking confidently.

A speech with short pauses: pause now and then if you are telling your audience a lot of information. It gives them time to remember what you say. It also helps them pay attention.

3

Third Idea for a Speech:

Your Body Language

Body language is when you use your body, not words, to communicate. You may use your hands, arms or eyes to make your speech more lively.

Why is body language important?

In a speech, body language helps us to keep the interest of our audience. Research tells us that the audience notices the body language of a person first, hears the tone of their voice second, then listens to the words.

Body language ... or not!

Imagine if you gave a speech without moving a muscle. The audience might find it boring or odd. Then imagine if you gave a speech using body language. You:

- walked around, looking at everyone in the audience
- held up your hand to show something or pointed at a chart or picture
- smiled at the audience.

This body language makes your speech more interesting and helps you connect with the audience.

5 Stop Speech Nerves

Tips to **Help** You

Everyone feels a little nervous before making a speech. That's normal!

Here are some tips to help you calm your nerves.

Colour Key Points

Colour parts of your speech to help you find key points quickly.

Speech Cards

1.

2.

Sometimes it can help to write your speech on small cards. Be sure to number them clearly.

Practise, Practise, Practise

Find a quiet place to practise your speech. It may help to practise in front of a mirror. The more you practise, the less nervous you will be!

PRACTISE!

Deep Breaths

Taking some deep breaths before you speak can really help to settle your nerves.

Health

Tummy Rumbles

Your tummy can make rumbling noises when muscles in your stomach contract. This often happens four or five hours after you have eaten. There's even a medical name for tummy rumbles: borborygmus!

"Oh, no, my tummy is rumbling!"

Smile

Before you speak, look at your audience and smile. A smile can help settle nerves. An audience likes to see a smile too.

Eat a Healthy Meal

Eat a healthy meal before you speak. That way, your tummy won't distract your audience by rumbling or growling!

Drink Water

Drink water before you speak. Fizzy drinks may make you burp!

Health

Burps

Burps are caused by swallowing air. Carbon dioxide gas in fizzy drinks can also cause burps. The loudest burp recorded was over 107 decibels. That's as loud as a chainsaw 100 metres away!

6 Speechwriting for a Prime Minister

Why Write **Speeches** for the **PM?**

The Prime Minister (PM) of New Zealand, John Key, is a very busy man. He does not have time to write his own speeches.

Instead, he works with a speechwriter who writes many kinds of speeches. The speeches might address school children, farmers, business workers or leaders of countries.

John Key

The PM's Speechwriter

The Prime Minister's speechwriter needs to be very good at three main things – researching, reading and writing.

John Key visits a kindergarten

John Key, the politician, liked the way his speechwriter wrote speeches. So, when John Key became Prime Minister, he asked that person to work as his only speechwriter.

The Prime Minister's speechwriter is busy every day. Often she works into the night to write the speeches on time.

Social Studies

John Key

John Key became Prime Minister of New Zealand in 2008. He often goes to schools to speak to children. In his spare time, he likes to be with his family, cook and play golf.

John Key

Meeting Before a Speech

Before a speech is written, the speechwriter meets with the Prime Minister and records what he says about the:

- **topic** of the speech
- **people** who will listen to the speech
- **main points** of the speech
- **date** he needs the speech by.

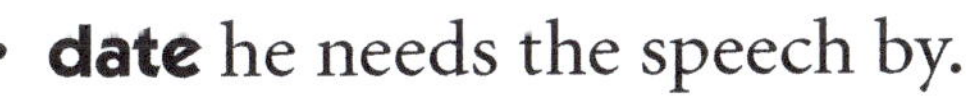

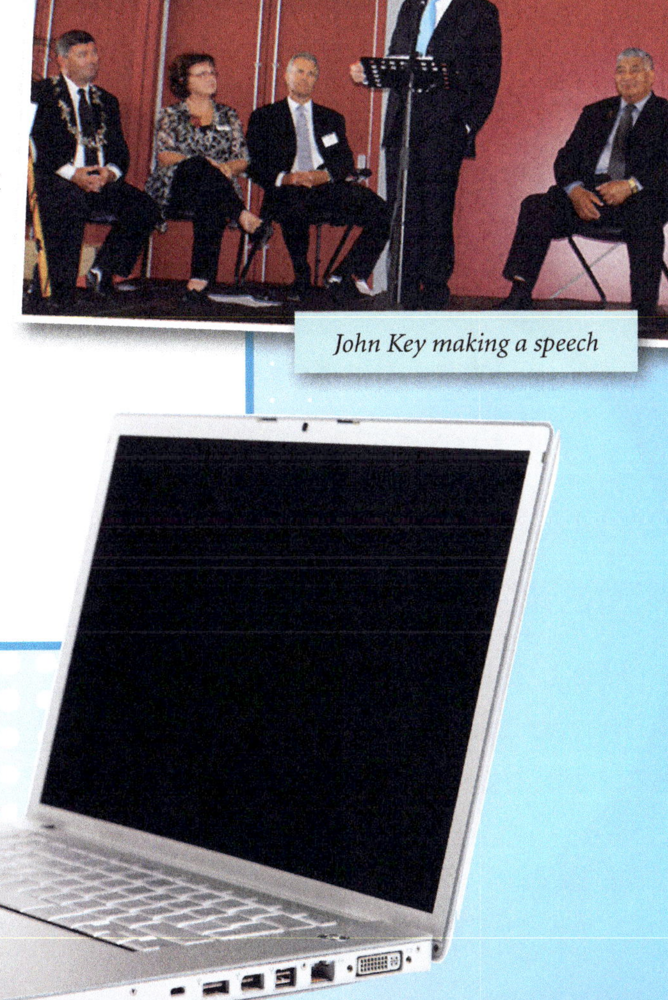

John Key making a speech

Writing the Speech

1

Research, Research, Research

The speechwriter spends many hours on research.

She makes sure that all the facts are correct. Then she is ready to write the first draft.

2

Write a Draft

The speechwriter writes the first draft of the speech.

Next, she proofreads and edits it. The draft speech is emailed to the Prime Minister to check.

Sometimes the speechwriter will meet with the Prime Minister to discuss it.

3

Write the Speech

The Prime Minister emails any text changes to the speechwriter.
She then writes the final speech.

The final speech is emailed to the Prime Minister in plenty of time. He likes to read it before he presents the speech.

4

Present the Speech

Now the Prime Minister is ready to present the speech.

He presents speeches to people in New Zealand or in other countries around the world.

Cycleway Project Speech

In 2009, John Key presented a speech about building a network of cycle tracks all over New Zealand, from Kaitaia to Bluff. Once the tracks are completed in about three years time, cyclists will be able to cycle from one end of the country to the other using various tracks.

John Key

KAITAIA

NEW ZEALAND

BLUFF

Index

Glossary

adaptation A version of a story that has been changed to use it in a different form of media

carbon dioxide A naturally-occurring gas that can be seen as the bubbles that make soft-drinks fizzy

decibels A scale used to measure the loudness of sound

Rottweiler A type of large dog, often used as a guard dog

summarise To briefly outline, at the end, the main points of a speech or presentation

tone The way a voice sounds (such as funny, serious, loud or soft)